NOW I KNOW WHY
I WAS CHOSEN

Written by: Maurice M Jenkins

Table of Contents

Acknowledgment

I would not have been able to reach here
without the presence of these two great people
in my life.

My mother, Darlene B. Davis, and my father, the
late Reverend Howard Lee Jenkins.

Chapter 1: Life

Life is a beautiful gift that all of us have been given by God. It's unpredictable for the most part. However, if there's one thing in our hands, it is how we choose to live it. As I pen down my thoughts on this piece of paper, I recollect my experiences and all that led me to write about them. Life has been nothing short of a package of surprises for me. Taking turns for the unfathomable is what life has been for me. My life has indeed been a roller coaster ride with its fair share of ups and downs. I'm sure you have faced your own share of hardships too. Unfortunately, pain is universal. However, it's not forever. My main motivation for writing this book is to help all of you see the light at the end of the tunnel.

We all have a certain purpose that we have been sent into the world for. More often than not, we fail to see that. We need to realize that everything that happens in our life doesn't happen as a mere coincidence. Instead, it happens under the guidance of that Supreme Power that created the Universe we reside in. The role that this Supreme Power plays in our lives is what I want to talk about in this book and help all of those struggling in one way or the other. When you don't feel that great or when something bogs you down, remember that you have a purpose to achieve. You have to do something important for which people will remember you for all times to come.

Every instance of my life is one where I have time and again felt divine intervention play a huge part. In situations where I had zero chances of survival, I lived. Why? Was that a mere coincidence? Well, it could have been! The first time, maybe? Or even the second time? But what about every time after that? Given what I went through and what I survived, labeling my experiences as a mere coincidence would be foolish. I could see the light, but yet I heard a voice telling me that I hadn't yet done what I was sent into the world for. I heard a voice tell me that I had a very important role to play, and at that moment, I knew I was going to live to do justice to that.

My friends, all of us have been sent into this world to fulfill a purpose. Unfortunately, when times are tough, we fail to realize that purpose. We are quick to give up and realize that this wasn't meant for us. Such moments are our greatest test. . Life isn't meant to be a bed of roses for any of us. Think of it this way, do you know a single person around you who doesn't have problems in their life? I don't. We all have our fair share of problems. But we need to realize that giving up is never an option. It never was for any of us.

For me, the meaning of life is reasonably simple. I believe that the ultimate goal is to reach eternal life with faith. When God calls me back to Him, I want to be in the best phase of my life. I want to be at a point in my life when my faith is at its peak. I want to have a personal relationship with Jesus, where He listens to everything I say, and I listen to everything He says. I want it to be a two-way relationship. My idea in life while I am here in this world is to be able to spread joy all around. I want to spread happiness and make sure that everyone around me also experiences some form of happiness when I am around them.

My life has given me very important lessons, and the most important of these is to never turn away from God. Remember that we are all people, whereas He is the Supreme Being, who has the power to control everything in the world. He is the one in whose hands lies the ultimate power. So we, as human beings, need to trust Him. We need to come to terms with the fact that He is the one who controls everything in life and hence can change things around for us as well. When most people encounter tough situations in life, that is when they tend to feel the most downtrodden. They lose hope and turn away from God too. That is the worst thing that you can ever do. God is our ultimate hope. When all else is gone, He remains. When no one helps you, He does. Believe that with conviction and see how much your life changes for the better.

There are so many instances in my life where I was about to lose myself. But what happened with me convinced me that God is there and He is watching over us. It convinced me that everything happens for a reason. We as human beings need to have full faith in that and understand that He is the ultimate controller of things. Things will only happen when He wants them to happen. The only way we can live a peaceful life is by making sure that we please Him in all ways possible. That is only possible when we do all we can to do good things. When we spread positivity around, it comes back to us. There are so many instances in my life where I witnessed all of this. I will be sharing most of the important incidents of my life to show you what I mean when I say God is in control of everything. In the Bible, he says, "Trust in the Lord with all your heart and do not lean on your own understanding. In all your ways acknowledge him, and he will make straight your paths" Proverbs 3:5-6. I believe in this verse more than anything. When we place all of our trust in the Supreme Being, he changes things for the better.

We are flawed beings. All of us have something or the other that makes us falter. But that is just how it was supposed to be as well. We weren't ever meant to be perfect. That is something that we need to understand here. But the way we choose to teach values is what matters. A very important lesson that life also taught me was to love everyone unconditionally. This most certainly does not mean that you should only love your friends. Love all of those too who have done bad to you or harmed you in any way possible. When you love those people as well, that is when you see all the love coming back. God loves you unconditionally and expects you to do the same.

Remember that you reap what you sow. So if you are mean to others, it will somehow come back to you in one way or the other. So you need to understand that for a fact and work towards becoming the best version of yourself slowly and gradually. It will surely take some time, but you will get there. According to the Bible, "Above all, love each other deeply, because love covers over a multitude of sins" I Peter 4:8. Here, we can see God telling us himself to spread love all around.

One of the toughest things for human beings is to forgive. The biggest life lesson for me is to forgive everyone. Today, I can safely say that I have a very pure heart, and I have forgiven all of those around me, even those who hurt me. When you forgive others, you let off a huge burden from your chest. You feel much better because you aren't carrying the weight of hatred. You learn to live a much more peaceful life when you forgive, which should surely be the ultimate goal. Even if you don't feel like forgiving someone, understand that this is what you should be doing because Christ wants you to do this. It all becomes easier when you have an unending love for Christ. Then you don't think about what you should be doing or what you feel like doing, but rather you think about what Christ would want you to do in different situations. According to the Bible, "So if you are offering your gift at the altar and there remember that your brother has something against you, leave your gift there before the altar and go. First, be reconciled to your brother, and then come and offer your gift" Matthew 5:23-24. Put Christ before yourself, and you will see how things automatically become much easier for you. He will make it much easier for you in no time.

One of the most important goals that I have in life is to help people get closer to God. Many people tend to lose hope when something bad happens to them. They tend to lose faith and have a pessimistic approach to life. This is possibly the worst thing that you can do to yourself. So when something bad happens, instead of moving away from God, we all should move closer to

Him, realizing that this is a problem we have, and only He can help us get out of it. Instead of losing faith, we should become stronger and ask for help from Him. I want to spread this message to as many people as I can so that everyone understands how important of a role God plays in our lives and how He is the one who can help us out of all situations. No matter how tough the situation is, God can help us out of it because He is the one whose hand vests ultimate power.

But then what we also need to understand is that we are the ones who should continuously keep asking from Him. It is only when we seek His love that we will get it. So in the Bible, God tells all of us to seek help from Him. He says that when we ask for it, He will surely give it to us. "Ask, and it will be given to you; seek, and you will find; knock, and it will be opened to you. For everyone who asks receives, and the one who seeks finds, and to the one who knocks it will be opened. Or which one of you, if his son asks him for bread, will give him a stone? Or if he asks for a fish, will give him a serpent? If you then, who are evil, know how to give good gifts to your children, how much more will your Father who is in heaven give good things to those who ask him!" Matthew 7:7-11.

Through this book, I want to make people come closer to God so that they understand the meaning of life and why we have been sent into this world. Through my relationship with God, I learned so much about Him and myself too. I believe that sharing my experiences will help so many people out there who are seeking guidance. My relationship with the

Supreme Being was not superb right from the start. I, too, lost hope many times. But what kept me going was God continuously making me realize that He is there. I could feel his presence now and then, and I loved every bit of it. Today, I am what I am because I have learned so much from God.

When I am alone, I speak to Him with full conviction, knowing that He listens to me. He tells me things, and I listen to Him too. I believe that it is that one-on-one connection that all of us need to build with our Lord. This connection goes a long way and helps us with many problems that we face in our lives. Not just that, but it also helps us understand ourselves in a much better way. One of the most important lessons that I learned in life was admitting that there is a problem and then having a solution-based approach to solve it. Whenever there was a problem, I always addressed it by having God as my confidante. I knew that if He was there with me and wanted to help me solve my problem, nothing stopped us. I believe that it was that faith that helped me through everything in my life.

What we need to do to make our connection with the Lord stronger is to let go of the negative energy. This negative energy consumes us, disallowing us to focus on the good in life. It rips us off all our energy and doesn't let us focus on the right things. We should be focusing on the good in life and understanding that any change for the better requires commitment and dedication. If you have made many mistakes in life, you don't need to worry. You can come to the right track in no time.

I know many people who say that they aren't willing to turn to God anymore because they have sinned a lot, and they feel like God will not listen to them. This is the worst approach to have. God created you, and no one loves you more than Him. The sooner we realize this, the better it is for us since we can then change our approach and become much better people. If you feel like you have sinned a lot, understand that God is there to forgive you. He is the Al-forgiving one. If you ask him for forgiveness, he will surely give it to you. You just need to have that conviction in your heart, and your intention needs to be pure. God wants you to turn to Him, so you can ask for forgiveness and turn to Him anytime you want. In the Bible, God tells us that he is there to forgive us and welcome us with open arms when we choose to go back to Him. "Whenever you stand praying, forgive, if you have anything against anyone, so that your Father who is in heaven will also forgive you your transgressions" Mark 11:25.

The main aim of writing this book is for me to help all of those around me who are struggling with their relationship with God. I want to share my experiences with them so that they understand how they can become better. The most important people in my life are my children and my grandchildren, and I teach them lessons like these too. I share my experiences with them, and they listen to me very carefully. I want them to live a successful and fulfilled life, which is something that is only possible if they establish that connection with God. It is that connection that will help them all their lives and will make them much better humans. Our relationship with God brings us closer to Him and makes our hearts softer, allowing us to be the best versions of ourselves.

Chapter 2: The Beginning

My journey starts very young. I was born into a Christian family. Everyone in my family was fairly religious, so you can say that I had a religious background right from the beginning. My grandfather, father, and uncles were all pastors. Having said that, I wasn't very close to God. We would go to church often, but I didn't have that drive to keep going. I knew what it meant to believe, but I didn't practice the teachings of my religion as much.

I started working in the family business from a young age because I wanted to support the family, as well as myself. I knew it was for the greater good and it kept me busy too. I was very busy with the happenings of my day-to-day life, and hence I didn't focus on my spiritual self. I rarely ever thought about God and all that He had planned for me.

I was engrossed in my everyday life about what I should be doing next. Since I was young, I wasn't really in the zone to pause and reflect on my life and what I was doing. I was almost always caught up in my own frenzy. It was only much later on that I realized so many things about myself. I realized what it was like to understand God and how there is a love language that exists between Him and us.

I lived in a rough neighborhood where there was always something or the other happening. There were many violent people there too, so I was naturally exposed to everything that was happening around me.

Since those were my formative years, I was greatly influenced by these events too. It was all I knew at the time so my learning was limited to that only. However, my grandparents guarded me and made sure that I didn't get into any trouble. They were always keeping an eye on me and told me that I should share things with them. I did exactly that because I knew that they were saying it for my good only, and they wanted me to be better than the people around me. This was life for me until I reached my teens and no major life lessons were learned. I was just protected by my grandparents, who tried to keep me on the right track always.

As a young child, I always lived a life where I felt the need to be accepted. I wanted others to accept me as I was. I wanted them to understand me. I had that thing at the back of my mind that I wanted to fit into society, and I was willing to go to any extent to make that possible. This meant that even if I had to do something bad to fit in, I would willingly do it. I didn't realize the effect that this could have on myself or my mental well-being in the long run. All I wanted was to fit in. That was my main goal. I had my grandparents mentor me quite often, but the truth is that I wasn't mature enough to understand anything at all at that time.

When I was younger, I partied a lot too, which all came as part of my wanting to fit in. I was just enjoying my life, and I had no bigger goal or ambition than just being in the moment. Apart from that, I also had people around me who enjoyed the same things. I didn't necessarily regret it. After all, who doesn't like partying? Of course, I enjoyed every bit of it. But there was one thing that I didn't have in my life at that stage - peace. No matter what I did, I felt like my soul was empty. I didn't have any relationship with God at that time. Yes, I did believe in Him, but there was nothing more than that.

My relationship with God developed further only when I grew much older and understood things in a better way. I understood what it meant to love God and speak to him. The things that I went through taught me the meaning of life and what it means to love. A few tragedies in my life made me really understand the meaning of life and where I was headed. But once I started developing that connection with God, I realized that there was no going back. The one thing that I loved the most about this was that it made me feel at peace on the inside. It made me feel like I had a purpose that I was working towards fulfilling. It didn't make me feel empty at all, and that is what I wanted to be able to improve my life for the better.

When I was living for others, there was always something that kept me at unease. There was always something that held me back because no matter what I did, I always felt that it wasn't enough. I was always left longing for more, and nothing seemed right at that moment. I knew that I had to do something to escape that cycle. When I started living for God, later on, everything seemed to fall into place perfectly. I loved this bond that I had formed with Him. I loved how it kept me afloat amidst everything that life chose to throw at me. More than anything, it gave me a purpose. It gave me a goal that I wanted to work towards. It gave me something to look forward to.

I realized that even the littlest things we do in life could please God. But pleasing people is the hardest thing ever. No matter what you do, you will always feel like you are missing something and that you need to keep striving for better. There is no end to it. The longing never ends. But with God, that is not the case. You can get whatever you want, and you can do whatever you want because God loves you unconditionally and is always there to forgive you no matter what you do. The Bible says, "9 This is how God showed his love among us: He sent his one and only Son into the world that we might live through him. 10 This is love: not that we loved God, but that he loved us and sent his Son as an atoning sacrifice for our sins. 11 Dear friends, since God so loved us, we also ought to love one another" John 4:9-11.

By now, you must be wondering about the life-changing moment that I experienced that brought me to this point. Well, it wasn't one moment that changed everything for me, as I mentioned earlier as well. Instead, it was an entire process. I transitioned into becoming a better version of myself each day as I grew closer to God and did things according to His will. I knew what I was doing was for the best and that I had to become better.

What really matters in my story were the dreams that I started getting. These played the most crucial role in my life. They changed everything for me. When I got these dreams, I felt like it was God speaking to me. I felt like He was trying to give me a message or say something to me. I felt like He was coming in my dreams and was helping me decipher the meaning of life - this was something that I hadn't been able to do for a very long time, so I felt that it was more of a divine intervention. It was the best thing ever for me, and it turned my life around like nothing else. It made me much smarter and much better as a person as well. It gave so much more meaning and depth to my life.

Many people feel that if they become "religious," they have to let go of a lot of things in life. This is the biggest misconception ever. When you turn to God, your entire lifestyle changes, but this most certainly doesn't mean that you have to stop doing things you love. It most certainly doesn't mean that you stop living your life. Instead, it means that you live a more meaningful life, where you have God with you in every decision that you make. It means that He is there to protect you and be by your side whenever you need Him. This is a bigger blessing than we can ever realize. It can make us understand all we need to know about devoting our lives to him. You don't have to be a monk to live a life like that. You don't need to cut out on everything that you do daily. You don't have to be a different person altogether. All you need to focus on is that you need to have a Supreme Being with you who can help you out with everything that you might need help with.

When he is there with you by your side, nothing can harm you. It is almost like this invisible sheet that goes with you wherever you go, protecting you from harm and giving you all the support you need. Sometimes when I look back at life, I wish I had realized this earlier. That would have really helped me start my journey much earlier on. But nonetheless, it is never too late. This again brings me back to why I am writing this book. You see, I am writing this book because I want everyone searching for meaning in their lives to turn to God at the soonest. He is the only being in the world who will never let you down and will be with you no matter what you do. He loves you unconditionally, and with His help, you can achieve anything that you want to.

If I reflect back on my good experiences, I can safely say that I had a wonderful life. I traveled all over Europe, enjoying my trip thoroughly. Why was I able to do that? I was able to do that because God loves me. He wanted to give me the best life. I was able to get all that I wanted and much more in life. I lived a life better than millions, and no matter what I do, I cannot thank God enough for giving me that life. I can safely say that it isn't only my good experiences that take me back to Him but also all the negative experiences since they remind me of Him and how He helped me through all of that. He allowed me to make memories to last a lifetime and also enabled me to remember Him enough by giving me all the bad memories too. I am thankful to him for each one of those memories.

Speaking of which, when making memories, we limit ourselves. We are the ones who tend to put a limit to the extent to which we can go. We believe there is so much we cannot do, which is exactly what limits us. We need to think beyond these limitations, and understand that this life is beautiful. There is so much that this life has to offer. It is only us who need to be able to see it. We need to understand that everything good is given to us by God only. We need to be thankful to Him for all that He has given us, and we need to work hard to make sure that He is pleased with us. The Bible says, "Behold, God is my salvation; I will trust, and will not be afraid; for the Lord God is my strength and my song, and he has become my salvation" Isaiah 12:2.

The most important part of my story that motivated me to write this book was my tragedies. I want to shed light on my strategies to help people understand that no matter what hardship comes our way, the last thing that we should be doing is losing hope. I will be talking about each of my tragedies one by one, with the main aim being that these tragedies can help you understand all of what I went through. I could have lost my life, but I lived through those moments. Why? Because God wanted me to live. I will talk about each of these stories one by one. You will realize that it was very hard to survive the things I did. The chances of survival in such situations are only minimal. But the fact that I lived through all of them shows that what happens only happens with the will of God, who is the ultimate controller of everything in life. Nothing happens without His willingness and consent. As the Bible says, "Do not be anxious about anything, but in every situation, by prayer and petition, with thanksgiving, present your requests to God. And the peace of God, which transcends all understanding, will guard your hearts and your minds in Christ Jesus" Philippians 4:6-7.

Chapter 3: Life in the Military

Another very important part of my life started when I joined the military. This was the phase of my life that taught me the most. From a very young age, joining the military was a dream for me. I wanted nothing more than to be living a life where I was serving my country while also doing all that I could to kick start my career. When I finally learned that I had gotten into the military, I was happier than I have ever been in my life. I couldn't believe it. I was over the moon. But I didn't know what awaited me on this road.

In the military, I met people from all walks of life-some rich, some poor. Living with those people taught me much more than any book or school could have ever taught me. It was like a game-changer for me.

In 1997, when I was on duty, I got shot in the head. It was the most painful experience of my life. I was screaming in pain the moment the bullet hit me. My first thought was that I would surely not be able to survive this. The excruciating pain was making it hard for me to breathe, let alone be able to think straight. I thought that I had lived a fulfilled life and that this was the end. But that was not it. I believe that the only reason why I am alive today is that God didn't want me to die at that point in time. I believe that if anyone else had been hit like that, there would have barely been any chances of survival. But today, here I am, living my best life, with no sign of being hurt like that at one point in time.

That was what strengthened my faith in God and drew me closer to Him. It made me reflect on so many things in life. People die in small car accidents or when they get sick too. I didn't die after being hit by a bullet like that! I thought I was going to die but I realized that it wasn't my time. Escaping death like that was the furthest thing from a coincidence. It made me realize that God's plan is the ultimate plan and that nothing can happen unless he wants it to happen. As the Bible says, "Trust in the LORD with all your heart and lean not on your own understanding; in all your ways submit to him, and he will make your paths straight" Proverbs 3:5-6.

This realization was what drew me closer to God and made me understand the real meaning behind being close to God. It made me realize what it means to have God by your side. From then on, I made sure that in whatever I did, I first got God's consent. After this incident, I started praying regularly, and I started asking God for things. I sought his help in all situations and made sure to ask Him before doing anything. He had been so kind to me, so I had to make sure that I did things that pleased Him as well. I wanted to be able to help myself by ensuring that I had His will in everything I did.

From then on, I can safely say that life only became better. More than anything else, I noticed that I was always at peace. I noticed that I was able to do things in a much better way. I was able to focus on things much better. Apart from that, I was also a much better person, as I noticed.

The one other thing I realized after being shot like that was that nothing happens till God doesn't want it to. I somehow believed that being shot in the head like that worked out in my favor since it brought me much closer to God than I ever thought I could get. It made me trust in His plans and realize that whatever He plans for us is the best plan there can ever be. I took some time to reflect on when that happened, and I realized that escaping something like this meant God didn't want me to die yet. He had some other plans for me, and I had to make sure I found out. He wanted me to live for a certain purpose. He wanted to fulfill certain things then, and I was determined to do so.

I drew closer and closer to God, and I couldn't be happier about it. Some people tend to lose hope when tragedies like this strike. They tend to lose faith in God. But what happened with me was quite the opposite. I was ever so grateful to God for blessing me with this life. Most people I know would have been dead if a bullet hit them like that. But with me, it was quite different. I was so happy that I was alive and breathing. But then I also knew that this wasn't for nothing. I had a purpose of fulfilling, and I wanted to do exactly that. I started trusting His plans more than anything, and I knew that He was the best planner. According to the Bible, "The Lord is not slow in keeping his promise, as some understand slowness. Instead, he is patient with you, not wanting anyone to perish, but everyone to come to repentance" Peter 3:9. This is one of the verses that I hold on to and remember when I feel like things aren't going my way. It makes me realize that things aren't always supposed to go my way. They are supposed to go God's way because He knows what is the best thing for me.

Chapter 4: More Tragedies

In 1988, around nine years before the incident in the military, I got spinal meningitis. While this was a very painful thing for me, it was also an eye-opener of sorts. It taught me what pain meant and how God was the only one who could reduce our pain since He is the one who controls everything. The Bible says, "Come to me, all you who are weary and burdened, and I will give you rest. Take my yoke upon you and learn from me, for I am gentle and humble in heart, and you will find rest for your souls. For my yoke is easy and my burden is light" Matthew 11:28-20.

So I only asked God for help during that time. I was admitted to the ICU for around two months, and I only kept remembering God through that time. That remembrance of God helped me get through this really tough phase in my life. It told me that only God could help me, and He was the only one I should beg for help from. His help surely came. The doctors had told me that my condition was worsening. But I kept telling myself that I would be okay only if God wanted me to. So I kept praying, asking Him to make things better for me. Things did eventually become better for me, and I couldn't be happier about it. God gave me yet another life to live. It wasn't my time to be called back, and so I lived through the hardship. But, again, e I was very happy with the way that God had helped me. I couldn't thank Him enough for being as kind to me as He was. The Bible says, "But when the kindness of God our Savior and His love for mankind appeared, He saved us, not based on deeds which we have done in righteousness, but according to His mercy, by the washing of regeneration and renewing by the Holy Spirit, whom He poured out upon us richly through Jesus Christ our Savior" Titus 3:4-6.

This again gave me the very important lesson that all pain that comes to us is inflicted by God. When He wants us to draw closer to Him, he does this by inflicting this pain on us, which makes us more and more inclined toward Him, asking only Him for help as we need it. When I came out from the hospital alive and healthy, I was ever so grateful to Him that I burst into tears on my way out. I started to see so much beauty in the little things of life- I noticed the birds chirping, I noticed the sun setting, and I couldn't be happier that God gave me another chance to live. When I was losing hope, I only asked Him for help, and help came. Slowly and gradually, this love story was developing between God and me. I asked Him for something; He gave it to me. I promised that I would never do anything that upset Him because He had been so very kind to me. I plainly rejoiced.

Then some time passed again. It was the year 2005 when I got into a fight with someone. He started abusing and then started hitting me too. To save myself, I had to hit back, and I got my jaw broken. Both sides of my mouth were broken, and I didn't understand what the issue was. I was in so much pain again, and I thought that this was the time that I would surely not be able to recover. I was mad at myself for getting into that fight in the first place. I should have just moved away instead of trying to save myself and getting hurt like that. I realized that God had saved me so many times, and this had happened again. This time around, I again thought that this was going to be the end and that I wasn't going to survive this at all. I got pneumonia for eight weeks. I thought that this time I was nearing death, and it was the end for me. But again, I slowly began to get better. I didn't understand how this happened and how God saved me each time. I was again so thankful to Him for helping me like that. Each time when I was in pain, I spent my time in remembrance of Him, knowing that this was what was going to help me out of this situation. I knew that this would help me with what I was struggling with as well.

Time and again, when something like this happened to me, I realized that this was God telling me that He wanted me to live through all of this. It was Him telling me that my time hadn't come yet, that I was going to continue to live, and that He was there for me each time. I used to tell these stories to everyone around me so that they would understand what God was capable of. I wanted to tell them how I was saved by God each time and how God loved me so much. I also wanted to give them the lesson of listening to God each time. I listened to God only, and I asked Him for help every time I got it.

I realized that my life had become so much better after I had become religious. It had become so much more sorted. I always did everything after I asked God for it. The Bible says, "The LORD will guide you always; he will satisfy your needs in a sun-scorched land and will strengthen your frame. You will be like a well-watered garden, like a spring whose waters never fail" Isaiah 58:11.

I realized that so many people understood my story and finally knew what it meant to ask God for help. That is what I wanted. I wanted to spread my message to as many people as possible to tell them that we have come into the world with a purpose. Till God doesn't want us to die, we will live. But we must live a fulfilled life. We must live a life where we continuously ask Him for guidance and do what He expects from us. We must live a life where we are always thankful for Him for what He has given us. This is very important for us to live a fulfilled life.

Then it was in the year 2008; I was visiting home in Mississippi. Soon after arriving, I headed out on the highway for some work. I got run over by a truck, and my leg got injured. I was in so much pain at that time. I thought that I had lost my leg for good this time. I couldn't fathom this. Tragedy had struck again. However, I tried to remain as patient as I could, despite my pain only increasing. I wanted to scream in my agony, but I remained calm and tried to keep my cool. I prayed to God to save me.

For the next two months, I had to get blood transfusions done. I had to stay in the hospital for long hours. But even during this time, I tried to remain as strong as possible. I told myself that this was what God had written for me and that I had to be pleased with whatever He wished for me. I was just glad that I didn't die because of this. The fact that I was on a bike meant

that I could have just come under the truck. But just
the fact that I was alive was something that I was so
thankful for. According to the Bible, "Oh come, let us
sing to the LORD! Let us shout joyfully to the Rock of
our salvation. Let us come before His presence with
thanksgiving; let us shout joyfully to Him with psalms.
For the LORD is the great God and the great King above
all gods. In His hand are the deep places of the earth'
the heights of the hills are His also. The sea is His, for
He made it; and His hands formed the dry land" Psalm
95:1-5.

Before this incident happened, I had a feeling in my
heart that something bad was about to happen. I felt
like I was going to get into an accident and that this
would be the final call for me. But just the fact that it
didn't happen was something that I was so thankful for.
I kept thinking about how God had blessed me and
how he had helped me out of so many situations that I
myself didn't even think I could come out of. I was so
happy that I couldn't contain my happiness. Indeed,
God is great. As the bible says, "Yours, O Lord, is the
greatness and the power and the glory and the victory
and the majesty, indeed everything in the heavens and
the earth; Yours is the dominion, O Lord, and You exalt
Yourself as head over all" Chronicles 29:11.

After this incident, things ran quite smoothly for me.
I kept thinking about life and what my purpose was in
this life. I kept thinking about how I could become a
better person and how I could live a meaningful life. I
wanted to live a life where I would work hard and
achieve things in life. I wanted to live a life where I

could please Jesus since He had been so kind to me. I wanted to spread my message to others so that they also understood what it meant to be close to God and how that could help each of us climb the ladder to success.

Sometimes, I felt that God wanted me to be close to Him, which is why He did all that He did. He wanted these hardships in my life to draw me closer to Him. Rightfully so, these hardships were what taught me the meaning of life. They taught me that only God has the power to do different things in life. No one apart from Him has ultimate control of things. No one apart from Him can do things in the right way. When He wants to bring His people closer to Him, He can inflict hardship upon them to realize that the only one they can count on is Him. To trust His plans and to be thankful for everything that He does is what life means to me now. The Bible says, "Let the peace of Christ rule in your hearts, since as members of one body you were called to peace. And be thankful. Let the message of Christ dwell among you richly as you teach and admonish one another with all wisdom through psalms, hymns, and songs from the Spirit, singing to God with gratitude in your hearts. And whatever you do, whether in word or deed, do it all in the name of the Lord Jesus, giving thanks to God the Father through Him" Colossians 3:15-17.

In 2021, only days after my birthday, I got stuck while pulling out my drive on my motorcycle. I was hurt so badly that my entire eye socket was bleeding. This time, I really thought that I would have to get admitted to the hospital again since I was bleeding so badly. But thankfully, that didn't happen. I rushed to the hospital and recovered the same night. Who could have ever thought something like this was possible? I was so thankful to God for not giving me a permanent injury. I could have lost my eyes that day. Merely the ability to see is such a gift from God. It is these little things that made me realize how much we have and how much we take for granted. It made me realize that we need to be more careful with the things we do. God has blessed us with so much, showing that He loves us a lot. We just need to be very thankful to Him for all we have. It is these little blessings that we don't even count as blessings that make the quality of our lives so much better. The sooner we understand this, the better it is for us. To quote the bible again, "Oh, give thanks to the LORD, for He is good, for His steadfast love endures forever! Let the redeemed of the LORD say so, whom He has redeemed from trouble and gathered in from the lands, from the east, and from the west, from the north and from the south" Psalm 119:1-8.

Then in the year 2022, I got divorced. When this was happening, I felt very sad because I didn't want any of this. But this is a story for which I have dedicated another chapter altogether, so I will shed light on this later on.

My idea for sharing all of these tragedies with everyone is that even in times when things don't seem to go our way, we shouldn't lose hope. We should know that God is always with us. He loved us more than anyone else and will never leave our side, no matter what happens. So it is on us to develop that relationship with Him. We need to spend some time reflecting on our lives. Only when we do that will we realize how much we have to be thankful for. Not just that, but we need to sit and speak to God in seclusion at times. We need to realize that He is the one who has been so kind to us, and so it is our turn to give back to Him and submit ourselves to Him. We must try to obey all of His commandments and do everything that pleases Him. The sooner we realize this, the sooner we can make our lives better. According to the Bible, "19 The acts of the flesh are obvious: sexual immorality, impurity, and debauchery; 20 idolatry and witchcraft; hatred, discord, jealousy, fits of rage, selfish ambition, dissensions, factions 21 and envy; drunkenness, orgies, and the like. I warn you, as I did before, that those who live like this will not inherit the kingdom of God" Galatians 5:19-21.

Even if you are an alcohol addict, you need to understand that it is never too late to stop. No matter what stage you are in life, you can always turn back. God is great. He will always forgive you. You just need to be the one to ask for forgiveness from Him, and He will surely give it to you. The joy and reward you will get in return for that are indeed unmatched. You just need to know that getting clean has many benefits. When you quit drinking, you become closer to God than ever. Not just that, but when you listen to God and what He has to say, you will always see how He gets back to you with the best things. You will see how things tend to turn out in your favor, always. God loves His people and is only waiting for them to turn back to

Him. According to the Bible, "Each of you should use whatever gift you have received to serve others, as faithful stewards of God's grace in its various forms. If anyone speaks, they should do so as one who speaks the very words of God. If anyone serves, they should do so with the strength God provides so that in all things, God may be praised through Jesus Christ. To him be the glory and the power forever and ever. Amen."

Chapter 5: Alcohol Addiction

Alcohol is the worst addiction that you can have. Anything that makes you lose your senses is the worst thing to do because then you are not yourself anymore. You do things that aren't right. I have come into contact with so many people who were alcohol addicts. They were such bright people, but their alcohol addiction ruined them. It made them do things that they should have never been doing.

What disturbed me the most was that they had become slaves to drinking. It was as if alcohol controlled their lives. They didn't know what they were doing. Many times, they did things they never would have done if they weren't under the influence. Later, when they realized what had happened, they were upset. There is no point in being upset about things when the damage is already done.

I look at it this way- when God has stopped us from something, there is definitely something behind it. God knows that it is bad for us, which is why He has stopped us from indulging in it. We need to understand His commandments and know that whatever He does is in our favor only. If we listen to Him, it will be for our own benefit only.

If you are an alcohol addict and are looking to quit, know that it is very much doable. Unfortunately, there is no one way of quitting drinking. However, here are a few tips that can help. You just need to find out what works for you. The idea is to start somewhere, at least, and slowly make your way up.

- **Examine Alcohol Health Effects**

The first and the most important thing you must do is to find out the adverse effects that alcohol has on your body. Understand how much it can damage you on the inside. This body that we are given is a gift by God. We need to value everything that he gives us. This reflects on us as individuals and how much we value what God gives us. The sooner we realize that what we take for granted is a blessing. We just need to make sure that we understand this. "Do not be anxious about anything, but in everything by prayer and supplication with thanksgiving let your requests be made known to God" Philippians 4:6.

- **Start with Moderation Management**

As a heavy alcohol drinker, it will surely be very hard to quit immediately. So what you must do is start with moderation management. Understand how you can slowly reduce your consumption and why that is good for you. Maybe you could start with a schedule. This can be tailored to your needs and should be as such that it matches your schedule. This way, you will at least be able to cut down on your consumption levels, which will help you cut down your overall intake.

- **Talk About It**

Talking about these things with your loved ones is always a great idea. They will provide you with encouragement and support. Not just that, but they will also be there to listen to you and make you feel better. Talking about your worries with someone helps as it gives you a fresh perspective and you feel more equipped to handle the problem after you're done venting. This can be anyone you're close to; your family, friends, etc. Tell them you're struggling but trying your best to overcome your addiction. Ask them for their support in this, and they will be there to help you.

- **Find A Community**

Look for others around who are also trying to deal with their alcohol addiction. When you form a community, you share things that the other person can relate to, allowing you to find comfort. Knowing that someone else is in the same boat as you, allows you to be more comfortable, which eventually also helps you manage your own addiction.

- **Know What to Say**

If you go somewhere and someone offers you a drink, don't give in to the sudden urge to have it. Tell them how you are focusing on your health and inculcating healthy habits. Your well-wishers will surely understand where you are coming from and will help you deal with this the right way. A refusal does not always have to be rude; remember that. You can just plainly tell them no and that this is what you think is best for your body. You also don't need to give a reason for it every time. You can just choose what you want and how you want it.

- **Change Your Environment**

The company you keep really affects your drinking habits. If you hang around with friends who are heavy drinkers, then you might feel the need to consume alcohol very often. It can make you give in very easily. If you feel like you lack self-control and being around such people makes things harder for you, then try to change your environment. It will surely be a breath of fresh air for you. Or you could even request them not to have alcohol when they're with you. If they're your true friends, they will understand where you are coming from and help you deal with it, instead of doing the opposite.

- **Find Another Drink**

Sometimes, you just need another drink to distract you. It could be anything you like. When you go out with your friends, you could just order that drink to help distract yourself a little- an orange juice, a mint margarita, an iced coffee, etc. With a dash of creativity, you are sure to find something that you like.

- **Keep Yourself Busy**

Have a routine that helps you stay occupied most of the time. This is important since it helps keep you distracted. For example, form a healthy gym routine, and keep yourself busy with work during the day. This can help you focus on the good things in life, and you might not even feel like having a drink. When you do productive things, you already feel so accomplished that it gives you another sense of high, keeping you away from all other things.

- **Prepare for Alcohol Detox**

You will feel certain symptoms when you cut down on your alcohol intake. These are a result of you being away from your addiction. It can give you anxiety, headaches, fatigue, insomnia, sudden mood changes, and even sweating. Understand that all of this is normal and that you should not worry about it. Don't get scared. It will take some time for these symptoms to go away, but you will surely get there sooner or later.

- **Practice Self Care**

Take care of yourself and focus on your well-being more than anything else. Understand that God only wants the best for us, which is why we must take care of ourselves. According to the Bible, "However, God is rich in mercy. He brought us to life with Christ while we were dead as a result of those things that we did wrong. He did this because of the great love that he has for us. You are saved by God's grace!" Ephesians 2:4-5.

⇒ When taking care of yourself, ensure you keep yourself well hydrated at all times.
⇒ Try to eat balanced meals to get all the nutrition you need.
⇒ Get into some form of physical activity so you remain fit.
⇒ Make sure that you get enough sleep to ensure that you are well-rested. Around nine hours each night is ideally recommended.

- **Rediscover Hobbies**

Try to get yourself busy with some hobbies. This can be anything that you like. Hobbies help you remain distracted, keeping your mind off of your addiction. For example, you could start working on DIY projects at home or inculcate a habit of reading. Not just that, but you could also volunteer to help others around you. These habits are productive and can help you focus on the good things in life.

- **Start Journaling**

Sometimes, letting it all out is what you need. Journaling helps you channel your innermost thoughts and pen everything down. Oftentimes, there are things that you do not want to talk about with anyone - not even the people who are closest to you. At times like these, you can pen your thoughts down. It will help you channel your thoughts and will also help you fix the problems that you are trying to manage. You could also start off by listing all the bad things that alcohol made you do. This could give you enough reasons to quit. For most people, journaling also helps give that instant boost of energy to keep going and do one's best.

- **Go to a Rehab Facility**

Not everyone can take alcohol addiction well. Even if they try to manage their addiction using different techniques, it doesn't always work out for them. In situations like these, you need to get professional help and go to a rehab facility. This isn't anything you need to beat yourself up over or feel bad about. Remember that you have an end goal; if you have to do something to get to that, you must do it. You can even find a therapist if that helps you. Sometimes, people also join online support groups because it makes them feel less alone and allows them to speak to people in the same boat.

What I want to stress is that you need to remember that this is a journey. It will surely not be easy. Sometimes, you might even want to give up. Understand that you need to be strong for your own self. You are doing this for your betterment, so you need to focus on the good here. Don't do things that you feel will weigh you down. Get that extra help you want, but make sure that whatever you do, you get one step closer to what you want to achieve.

What I always tell others around me is that if God has told you to abstain from something, it is most definitely for your benefit only. God loves His people more than anything else, which is why it is binding upon us to listen to his commandments and understand where He is coming from. This is very important to help us keep going. In the Bible, God says, "Come to me, all of you who are tired from carrying heavy loads, and I will give you rest. Take my yoke and put it on you, and learn from me, because I am gentle and humble in spirit; and you will find rest" Matthew 11:28-29. He tells us that he is there for us and will help us through everything that is bothering us. This is why we need to make sure that we do things that He wants us to do.

Anything that comes out of alcohol addiction is bad- either it makes you do wrong things, or it turns you into someone you are not. God is All-knowing, and so if

He had told us to stay away from something, there is a very strong reason behind it. Thus, we must obey Him.

Chapter 6: Love and Marriage

Finding love is indeed the most beautiful thing ever. To know that there is someone who cares for you and prioritizes you above all else can feel beautiful and overwhelming. To have someone with whom you can share your life, knowing they are honest with you, is something everyone craves. The same was true for me too.

As a teenager, I always had this fancy idea of getting married. I always wanted to meet that one true love of my life, with whom I could spend my whole life. My idea of love was that when it is right, you just know it. So, I had this feeling that the day it just clicked, I would know she was the one.

I got married thrice in my life. Unfortunately, none of my marriages worked out. However, I want to tell each of you that there is nothing wrong with that. We chose to separate because we knew that we weren't heading anywhere, and it was important for us to live fulfilled lives, which we couldn't do while we were still together. We weren't adding any value to each others' lives, and we knew that it was best that we headed our separate ways.

When I met my first wife, I thought she was the one. I fell in love with her instantly, and I wanted to do everything I could to make her happy. The first few years went well, but slowly and gradually, things started getting toxic. We just weren't happy with each other, and both of us were in unanimous agreement on this. So, we decided that we should end it, and so we did. The same happened with my other two wives. It just didn't work out with any of them.

As much as I was in love with the idea of 'love,' it just didn't work out for me the way I had hoped it would. Initially, it was very heartbreaking. I grieved a lot when each of my marriages ended because I wanted them to work out. Who doesn't like having a nice spouse? Who doesn't like to come home to a beautiful family waiting for them? I tried as hard as possible to make sure my marriages were successful. I did all I could, but when I finally realized that there was no chance, I knew it was time to part ways. In no way will I say that any of my wives were bad. It was just that things did not unravel for us the way we had imagined. Like me, my wives also tried their best to make things work, but it just wasn't happening.

When my third divorce happened, I was devastated because it seemed all of my relationships were failing. There was a point where I had lost hope. But then I realized that if this was what God had destined for me, I had to make my peace with it and be happy. God always knows what is best for us, and if something happens that bogs us down, we need to understand that we need to be happy in God's will. In the Bible, God says, "So we do not lose heart. Though our outer self is wasting away, our inner self is being renewed day by day. For this light momentary affliction is preparing for us an eternal weight of glory beyond all comparison, as we look not to the things that are seen but to the things that are unseen. For the things that are seen are transient, but the things that are unseen are eternal" Corinthians 4:16-18.

So I told myself that if this was it, I had to accept this as the truth and have faith that there is something behind each of God's plans. I told myself I would be happy with whatever God decided for me without losing hope. Sometimes, no matter how hard we try, if things aren't meant to work out, they don't. When this happens, we lose hope very fast without realizing that God loves us more than anyone else and that He wouldn't have anything planned for us that doesn't work out in our favor. We don't know what is good for us, but He surely does and will always be there to help us through it all.

When I got divorced the third time, I started to realize that our eternal love will always be God, which is why we need to devote ourselves to Him entirely. We need to realize that He is the one who loves us the most and is the one with whom we should form an unbreakable bond. He is the one who will always be there to help us, no matter what happens. When my connection with God became even stronger, I realized that I was becoming much calmer and was more at peace. It was that connection with God that told me that things would turn out for the better.

Of course, it is beautiful to find love in someone and have someone to share the rest of your life with. But I realized that if it wasn't working out, then God had something bigger planned for me. He knew what was best for me and was slowly getting me there. I was holding on to hope tight, knowing that God was the one to help me through everything in life. Today, I can safely say that I have no hard feelings for my wives. I count my divorces as life-changing experiences that changed me for the better and made me a better person. They made me realize so many things, again teaching me the importance of having unwavering faith and believing in God, knowing that He will never plan anything for us which isn't in our favor. In the Bible, God tells us how much he loves us. He says, "No, in all these things we are more than conquerors through him who loved us. 38 For I am convinced that neither death nor life, neither angels nor demons, neither the present nor the future, nor any powers, 39 neither height nor depth, nor anything else in all creation, will be able to separate us from the love of God that is in Christ Jesus our Lord" Romans 8:37-39.

From then on, I was on a path to self-discovery, where I realized so many things about myself. I told myself that the eternal goal was to make God happy and form a relationship with Him since that is the only relationship that is indeed everlasting. That is the only relationship that never dies. Today, when I think back, I see so much good in whatever God planned for me. I see how much He loves me, and I see His reasons for everything too. The key is to speak to God and understand what He says. The key is to remain so close to him that we understand everything He tells us in the Bible. For me, the Bible is a book that I choose as my guide in life. Whenever I feel distraught, I read the Bible and understand God's commandments. I try to understand what God wants to tell me. Through the Bible, I feel like God is speaking to me.

While my marriages didn't last, I have children with two of my wives. My children are truly my biggest blessings. As of today, I am a grandfather too, and the people I love the most are my grandchildren. My ultimate goal is to give them all these life lessons and make them understand what it means to form a connection with God- the Eternal Being. I want my grandkids to understand the meaning of unwavering faith and undying love. God's love is the only love in our lives that can never die. In the Bible, God tells us, "Know therefore that the Lord your God is God; he is the faithful God, keeping his covenant of love to a thousand generations of those who love him and keep his commandments" Deuteronomy 7:9.

My last marriage ended in January 2022, and ever since then, I have been trying to be strong and am trying to strengthen my connection with God further. I believe that this is the ultimate goal that I have in my life. My Lord is my strength, and He is the one I hold on to whenever I feel like I am grieving. I always try to look at the bright side of things, so I can safely say that my failed marriages made me a much stronger person and made me realize that not everything is for everyone. It made me realize that God is the ultimate power in the world, and everything happens for a reason. I try to think of reasons why my marriages didn't last, and all I can say is that it was what God thought was best for me. Maybe he wanted me to become much closer to Him or to become a better person, so I did. We will never understand what is good for us. Only God is all-knowing, so we should know that whatever he plans for us will always be for the better. My failed marriages turned me into a better human being. Maybe God wanted it that way - that is how I think of it.

Remember that it is on us to inculcate a positive mindset and try to find the good in everything that happens to us. It is very easy to lose hope and not understand things well. What is hard is trying to understand things correctly, keeping God as the center of our focus. In the Bible, God says, "For to us God revealed them through the Spirit; for the Spirit searches all things, even the depths of God. For who among men knows the thoughts of a man except the spirit of the man which is in him? Even so the thoughts of God no one knows except the Spirit of God" Corinthians 2:10-11.

It most certainly is great to find love. When you find the right person in your life, it becomes more beautiful. Your life partner is there for you in your happiness and sadness. When things weren't working out for me, I did whatever I could to change that. But when I couldn't, I told myself that God probably had something else planned for me. I told myself that nothing happens unless God wants it to, and it was best to accept that. No matter how hard I try, if God doesn't want it, it won't happen.

I keep reminding myself that the most permanent relationship we have is the one we have with God because he is Eternal. His love for his beings is unmatched, and the sooner we understand that the sooner we can make our lives more meaningful. To all the young people looking for love, you are on the right track. Nothing is more beautiful than finding solace in someone you can share your whole life with. It makes your life much more beautiful because you have so much to look forward to.

Here, I have compiled a list of important tips that can strengthen your relationship.

Tips for a Lasting Marriage

It might not seem very befitting to get marriage tips from someone who has had three failed marriages in life. But let me tell you, nothing can teach you more than experience. When one learns from their own experience, guiding others becomes so much easier. I attribute my failed marriages to destiny, and what God wanted for me because he thought it was best. Only God knows what is best for us.

The union of two people who bring out the best in each other is, I believe, one of the most beautiful things in the world. These tips will surely be very helpful for you.

- **Spend Time With Each Other**

In today's busy life, spouses rarely spend quality time together. Spending time together doing something productive or simply speaking to each other establishes a strong connection and allows the two to be connected at a deeper level. I cannot stress enough how important it is to make a deliberate effort to find that time for each other. I agree that it can be quite challenging these days, and both spouses might find themselves stuck with daily chores and work. But nothing can be more important than your relationship, right? So no matter how busy you are, spend time together and speak to each other about the smallest things. Both partners should know what is happening in each other's lives- scheduled date nights, weekend activities, and dinners at home are a part of this. Make time for each other and see how your relationship grows. In the Bible, God repeatedly talks about love and marriage and how he created humans in pairs. He says, "So God created man in his own image, in the image of God he created him; male and female he created them. And God blessed them. And God said to them, 'Be fruitful and multiply and fill the earth and subdue it and have dominion over the fish of the sea and over the birds of the heavens and over every living thing that moves on the earth'" Genesis 1:27-28.

- **Communicate Openly**

Your spouse is your significant other, right? You need to speak to them about whatever is going on in your mind. Be very open about what you are thinking. This person is your life partner. You have to spend your whole life with them. So you must speak to them about everything that is on your mind. Open communication allows healthy discussions, which is very important for a healthy relationship. If there is something on your mind that is bothering you, speak to your spouse about it. Ask for their opinion on it. Not only does this allow you both to solve your issues, but it also makes the other feel valued. When you discuss problems, you both give each other the importance and respect you deserve. Marital satisfaction is very important, and that only comes when you speak openly about whatever is going on in your head.

- **Solve Issues at the Earliest**

Problems can arise in any relationship - be it from miscommunication, misunderstanding, or difference of opinion. It is only normal to find yourself being upset with your spouse over something. The key is to solve all problems at the earliest. When you sleep over your problems and let them persist, the wounds only become deeper. It is never wise to stretch issues. Solve them at the earliest. Make sure to speak to your partner about what is bothering them too.

In most cases, ego plays a huge part in making problems worse. Most people wait for their partners to make the first move, which is the worst thing you can do for your relationship. Remember that you both took this decision to be with each other in good and bad, so whatever the situation, you need to be the first to speak about it and solve it. The longer the problem persists, the greater the chances of it getting worse. You have to spend your whole lives with each other, so speak about everything and solve issues right when they arise.

- **Accept Your Partner for Who They Are**

Everyone is different. Everyone has a different personality. When you marry someone, you should truly accept them as they are, with their flaws. Never try to change your partner. When you enforce things on them, they feel caged, which is very unhealthy for your relationship. It makes the relationship extremely toxic. Instead, accept them for who they are, with their strengths and weakness. These are the things that make them unique. Accept that, embrace their faults, and you'll see how happy you'll be.

- **Learn to Forgive**

We are all human and thus highly prone to making mistakes. When your partner makes a mistake, be quick to forgive them. The last thing you should be doing is holding anything against them or reminding them of their mistake over and over. That can make them feel very sad and upset and can damage your relationship. If they have done something that hurt you, make it very clear to them. Communicate openly and tell them that it hurt you and that they should not do it again. But forgive them and forget about it too. When we learn to look past our mistakes, that is when we grow and take our relationship to the next level.

- **Find Out What Your Common Interests Are**

You must find out what your common interests are. When you do that, it allows you to spend quality time together and do things that both of you enjoy. Explore things together and see what you like and vice versa. When you do that, you naturally learn how to please each other.

- **Respect Each Other**

Nothing is more important than respect in a relationship. When you truly love someone, you respect them. Even if there is something, you disagree with or don't like, speak to them about it. Never utter bad words, or malign them. It only makes them feel bad about themselves, eventually tarnishing the relationship's roots. Both partners need to have dignity in conduct. Respect who they are, how they feel, and what they do. This is the basis of a healthy relationship and allows you to build something great together.

God has repeatedly stressed the importance of love in a marriage, which only comes from respect. He says, "And over all these virtues put on love, which binds them all together in perfect unity. Let the peace of Christ rule in your hearts since you were called to peace as members of one body. And be thankful. Let the message of Christ dwell among you richly as you teach and admonish one another with all wisdom through psalms, hymns, and songs from the Spirit, singing to God with gratitude in your hearts. And whatever you do, whether in word or deed, do it all in the name of the Lord Jesus, giving thanks to God the Father through him" Colossians 3:14-17.

- **Trust Each Other**

Trust is the foundation of a healthy relationship. When your partner tells you something, believe them. Trust allows both of you to feel safe and connected. Remember, the two of you are a team. Since marriage is a lifetime commitment, there needs to be mutual trust. If you don't trust each other and keep a check on each other continuously, that just goes on to show how the foundations of your relationship are very weak.

- **Know Yourself First**

To form a healthy relationship, you must try to understand yourself first. The process of growth never stops. For a healthy relationship, you need to work on your flaws and try to become the best version of yourself. Find out what your weaknesses are, and work on them. For example, if you have anger issues, try to work on those. Anger issues can destroy a relationship because they can lead you to act in the worst way possible. When you learn things about yourself, you will also understand your partner better. That will help you see where they are coming from, their dreams, and where they wish to get in life. A lifelong commitment requires you to understand each other, and that can only happen when you understand yourself first.

- **Support Each Other's Dreams**

Learn about where each of you wants to get in life and support each other. When you do that, you grow together as a team. Be each other's backbone. If you think you can help your partner get a step closer to their dreams, do that. You both are committed to each other for life, so you must be there for each other at all times. Ambition drives you and allows you to look ahead in life. There is nothing more rewarding than having an ambitious partner in your life.

Support your partner in reaching for the stars, and you will only see how they reciprocate it. Time and again, God has stressed the importance of marriage as a relationship, so we must work hard to do our part. In the Bible, God says, "'Haven't you read,' he replied, 'that at the beginning the Creator 'made them male and female,' and said, 'For this reason, a man will leave his father and mother and be united to his wife, and the two will become one flesh? So they are no longer two, but one flesh. Therefore, what God has joined together, let no one separate" Matthew 19:4-6.

- **Never Compare to Other Couples**

The only person you should be comparing yourself to is your own yourself. When you compare your relationship to someone else's, it only causes more complications. It brings envy into the relationship, which is hazardous for you. If something about your partner bothers you, speak to them about it and try to improve. Grow together as a couple. When you compare yourself to others, it only destroys you. Every couple has different dynamics and problems that you aren't aware of. So never try to be like someone else, or copy what they do. That will be extremely hazardous for both of you and your relationship.

- **Do Your Duties Rightfully**

A marriage is a partnership where you have certain duties and obligations to carry out. Sort these out amongst yourselves and come to a resolution. Once you are on the same page, ensure you perform all your duties correctly. Never lag behind and always let each other know about what is happening. Doing that tells your partner that you are honest in the relationship and that you value your commitments. This helps build a strong relationship that lasts.

- **Focus on Intimacy**

The physical connection between spouses is a very important part of the marriage. This does mean not only sexual connection but also includes emotional intimacy. Your partner should be able to come to you and be open about how they feel. They should be able to share their dark side with you too, and you should be open to that. Also, explore sexuality and learn about each other's sexual needs. Make a conscious effort to be as attractive to your partner as possible. That will draw them closer to you and help form that strong connection between you both. God has repeatedly spoken in the Bible about the sexual connection between spouses. He says, "But because of the temptation to sexual immorality, each man should have his own wife and each woman her own husband. The husband should give to his wife her conjugal rights, and likewise the wife to her husband. The wife does not have authority over her own body, but the husband does. Likewise, the husband does not have authority over his own body, but the wife does. Do not deprive one another, except perhaps by agreement for a limited time, that you may devote yourselves to prayer; but then come together again, so that Satan may not tempt you because of your lack of self-control" Corinthians 7:2-5.

- **Have Patience**

Good things come to those who wait. Both partners must never rush into anything. It is important to listen to each other and understand where each of you is coming from. When you do that, you increase your chances of making better decisions in life, which is extremely important. Our shortcomings usually lead us to act rudely or harshly in situations we cannot control. This is what leads to failed marriages. It is always important to wait. If your spouse makes a mistake, don't be quick to lash out at them. Give it some time. If they have made a mistake, they will surely realize it and will come back to you with an apology. If you think you are doing something wrong, wait it out and think about it patiently. You will surely see where you are at fault, which will help you grow out of it.

- **Be Friends Before Anything Else**
 More than anything else, be friends. You must spend your whole life with your spouse, so you must understand them and be friends with them. You can only enjoy spending time with them when you laugh together and share things. Never keep secrets from each other, and speak about even the smallest of things. Explore new places together and travel together too. Find solace in each other's company. That will allow you both to grow over time.

- **Be Loyal to Your Partner**
 Loyalty in a relationship is extremely important. More than anything, a marriage is a lifelong commitment. This means that you must be very loyal to your partner and should never even think about cheating on them. A marriage is a very pure and chaste relationship, the importance of which has been stressed over and over in the Bible. God says, "Husbands, love your wives, as Christ loved the church and gave himself up for her, that he might sanctify her, having cleansed her by the washing of water with the

word, so that he might present the church to himself in splendor, without spot or wrinkle or any such thing, that she might be holy and without blemish. In the same way, husbands should love their wives as their own bodies. He who loves his wife loves himself. For no one ever hated his own flesh, but nourishes and cherishes it, just as Christ does the church" Ephesians 5: 25-29. Always be mindful of the marriage vows you made. Understand that God chose this person to be your life partner, and so you ought to be truthful to the relationship. You must always take care of your partner and never think of anyone else besides them. For a marriage to work out well, you must be true to your word.

- **Learn to Compromise**

A marriage is a partnership between two people who decide to spend their life together. Of course, there will be challenges and obstacles in the way. You must learn how to compromise at times. Being too uptight will only harm your relationship. You mustn't always expect things to go your way. Sometimes, you must give in to what your partner is saying. It is a two-way relationship that will only work out well when the two of you decide to give in sometimes. Try to find common ground. This doesn't mean that you give up on your dreams. It only means that you understand your partner and be flexible at times. Try to put yourself in their shoes. Only then will you understand them and what they are saying.

- **Value Your Spouse**

Your spouse should know that they are the most important person to you. To value them that way means that you listen carefully to what they say. It means that you take care of their needs and understand them. It also means that you enjoy every moment together. It is every little act that counts. Your spouse should know that you truly care for them and would be willing to go to any extent needed for them.

- **Give Each Other Space**

Space is very important for any relationship to grow. Spending time allows both partners to keep that spark alive in the relationship. Spend some time doing things you like, and let your partner do the same too. Being too clingy can be annoying and also toxic to some extent. When you both take out time to do things you love, it will keep the freshness alive. It also shows how much you trust each other. If your spouse wants to go out with their friend and have fun, let them. It fosters strength and independence and doesn't make the other person feel like they're caged. Orbuch researched marriage and divorce. The project was called The Early Years of Marriage Project. She reported that 29% of spouses felt that they had little to no privacy in the relationship, which was a major contributor to an unhappy marriage. When asked why space is so important in a relationship, she emphasized having your own set of interests and friends along with getting some alone time. This helps you and your partner feel happier and less bored. Spending time with yourself also allows you to process your thoughts and relax. It allows you to be your own person and not be completely defined by your partner.

- **Think About What Life Would Be Like Without Them**

Having a good spouse is a huge blessing. If you keep reminding yourself of how lucky you are to have them in your life, you will surely be much happier in your relationship and will value them for who they are. It will keep reminding you of how much they do for you and how much beauty they add to your life. When you try imagining your life without them, you will surely make that extra effort to ensure they are happy. When your partner sees that extra effort from your end, they will do the same. This will surely lead to a more blissful relationship. God has time and again stressed on love between spouses. In the Bible, God says, "Love is patient, love is kind. It does not envy, it does not boast, it is not proud. It does not dishonor others, it is not self-seeking, it is not easily angered, it keeps no record of wrongs. Love does not delight in evil but rejoices with the truth. It always protects, always trusts, always hopes, always perseveres" Corinthians 13:4-7.

- **Seek Professional Help if Needed**

It is natural to have problems in your marriage. You both stem from different backgrounds and have different outlooks on life. Try to understand each other and resolve conflicts when they arise. However, if you still feel like the problems persist and that you aren't able to come to a common ground, seek professional help. Seeking professional help is still seen as a taboo in many cultures and countries. However, you need to understand that nothing is more important than your relationship. There is nothing wrong with having someone help you resolve your differences. You can go to a relationship counselor who will take you through steps that can help you understand life much better. Not just that, but they will also help you understand each other much better. If you think you need marriage counseling, get it. Don't overthink it. To make a relationship work, you must keep working for it, and you will eventually see how things get better with time.

- **Don't Strive for Perfection**

We are all human, and there is no such thing as 'perfection' in our lives. The sooner we understand that, the sooner we can make life simpler. You are not perfect, and neither is your partner. So you need to stop expecting too much from them. We all make mistakes, and we need to embrace that. Always strive to become better, but never try to achieve perfection. When you do that, you will always find yourself dissatisfied with what you have. Try to see the good in everything around you and live in the present. To achieve a perfect future, most people tend to destroy what they have in the present, which only causes more problems and discontentment in a relationship. Appreciate your partner and see the little things they do for you. See how they are also trying to be the best version of themselves for you. When you do that, you will see that perfection is nothing but a state of mind and appreciate your partner for who they are.

- **Know The Don'ts of the Relationship**

Both partners should be aware of some deal breakers in a relationship. There are some things that people don't like under any circumstances. Make sure you know what those are for your partner, and don't venture there or try and test them. When you got married to this person, you made a vow to be with them through thick and thin, so know what the deal breakers are, to value your relationship. Make sure your partner also knows about what you don't appreciate so that you both can work towards a healthy relationship. Marriage is all about healthy teamwork. It is one of the purest relationships that exist. God says, "Two are better than one because they have a good reward for their toil. For if they fall, one will lift up his fellow. But woe to him who is alone when he falls and has not another to lift him up! Again, if two lie together, they keep warm, but how can one keep warm alone? And though a man might prevail against one who is alone, two will withstand him-a threefold cord is not quickly broken" Ecclesiastes 4:9-12.

- **Come to Common Grounds**

It is very common for spouses to have different opinions on things. However, what is important is that you both try to meet midway so that you can easily make big decisions in life. For example, you must be on one page about how many kids you want. Decisions like these are massive and dictate how you spend your whole life. So you must try to put your point forward to your partner. In the same way, they must put their point across to you, and then you should meet somewhere in the middle so there is no confusion.

With these tips, you can surely make your marriage work. Remember, teamwork makes the dream work.

First, you need to invest in your relationship and understand your partner. Every relationship has different dynamics. You understand your relationship better than anyone else, so focus on it and try to become better each day.

As a retired US Army Veteran, I can say that I was very uptight in my life. That was what I had been trained to be like, and I didn't realize that it was not good for my relationships. Similarly, analyze your situation and understand where you lack. Once you're aware, try to work on your weaknesses one at a time, and you will see the improvement in no time.

Marriage is beautiful. To have someone who loves you unconditionally is the best feeling in the world. Make sure to cherish that and celebrate each day of your life with your partner.

Chapter 7: Important Lessons from Life

Life is a gift from God. It is truly a blessing that we have. Come to think of it this way, there are so many people fighting for their lives in hospitals. They want to live, but they don't have time. So many people are going through mental illnesses, unable to keep up with their burdens. So the fact that we are here living our lives is nothing short of a blessing. Every day, we should thank God for what He has given us.

In the Bible, God says, "But if God so clothes the grass of the field, which today is alive and tomorrow is thrown into the oven, will he not much more clothe you, O you of little faith? Therefore, do not be anxious, saying, 'What shall we eat?' or 'What shall we drink?' or 'What shall we wear?' For the Gentiles seek after all these things, and your heavenly Father knows that you need them all. But seek first the kingdom of God and his righteousness, and all these things will be added to you" Matthew 6:30-33.

Despite all that I went through in my life, I am still very thankful to God for everything He has given me. I have learned a lot of valuable lessons in my life, and I want to share all of these with you so that you can benefit from them.

1. **Always be Thankful**

No matter what life throws at you, always be thankful for what you have been blessed with. Hardships are a part of life that should only make us strong. They should bring us close to God rather than take us away from Him. As I have shared several times in this book, there have been multiple instances where I almost lost my life. I was in severe pain too. Some of it was physical, but other times, it was emotional pain, as well. As I have said before, I went through a lot of emotional turmoil in my life because of my divorces.

But I didn't let any of that break me. On the contrary, I was and am still very thankful to God. Everything in my life has brought me closer to God and has shown me what it means to develop a bond with God. It has shown me how God chose me for a greater purpose and how He was the one to pull me out of every difficult situation in life.

Research has shown that being thankful also leads to positive emotions, which helps us feel good and build strong relationships. In the Bible, God has repeatedly stressed the importance of being thankful and why that is important for us. He says, "Let the peace of Christ rule in your hearts since you were called to peace as members of one body. And be thankful. Let the message of Christ dwell among you richly as you teach and admonish one another with all wisdom through psalms, hymns, and songs from the Spirit, singing to God with gratitude in your hearts. And whatever you do, whether in word or deed, do it all in the name of the Lord Jesus, giving thanks to God the Father through him" Colossians 3:15-17.

2. Believe in the Power of Prayer

It is also essential to believe in prayer and to ask God to give us what we want. Remember that no one loves us more than God does. So no matter what happens in life, we should ask God for what we want, with the utmost belief that He is listening and will surely give us the things we ask of him. When we pray to God and humbly submit ourselves to Him, there is no way that we won't get what our heart desires.

But when you do so, do it with the belief that God is listening. We are humans with barely any power to control our lives. It is He who has made us and knows what is best for us. So we must listen to him and understand Him too. Then, when God sees us bow down to Him, He will know how much we love Him.

I went through so much hardship, and the only thing that helped me throughout this time was holding on to God's helping hand. I noticed that everything became so much better for me then. I was able to get what I wanted without any issues. When I asked God for help, I asked Him to give me what was better for me because only He knows what is best for us. We think we know what is best for us, but we don't. We can't see the future, but since God is All-knowing and Ever powerful, He knows what is best for us.

In the Bible, God says, "For I know the plans I have for you, declares the Lord, plans for welfare and not for evil, to give you a future and a hope. Then you will call upon me and come and pray to me, and I will hear you. You will seek me and find me when you seek me with all your heart. I will be found by you, declares the Lord, and I will restore your fortunes and gather you from all the nations and all the places where I have driven you, declares the Lord, and I will bring you back to the place from which I sent you into exile. Because you have said, 'The Lord has raised up prophets for us in Babylon" Jeremiah 29:11-15.

If you haven't gotten into the habit of praying, then you can do it now. It is never too late to turn to God. He is always waiting for us to turn back to Him because He loves us more than we can ever imagine.

3. Never Lose Hope

It is also very important to have an optimistic approach to life. We must never lose hope, no matter how bleak the situation is. Remember that God has the power to turn everything around. With His command, everything can change in one instant. Therefore, we must always try to look at the bright side of the situation. Even in the darkest days of my life, when I was in the hospital bed, not knowing how my life would turn out, I was hopeful. There were days when I felt mentally exhausted and failed to see the good in life, but I made a deliberate effort to at least try. I tried to tell myself that God is the best planner and that He surely has something great planned for me.

Losing hope means losing faith in God's ability to change things. When times are rough, tell yourself that this too shall pass. Despite all the hardships we face, we must remember that God is there to help us through everything. Try to see the light at the end of the tunnel. I know how hard it can be when things don't seem to be turning out the way we wanted them to. But understand that hardships are a part of life. They help us turn to God and so we mustn't lose hope. We should always hope and pray that things work out for us. God will only help us when He sees us make that extra effort too. He will only change things for us when we pray and ask Him for help.

In the Bible, God says, "Therefore, since we have such a hope, we are very bold. We are not like Moses, who would put a veil over his face to prevent the Israelites from seeing the end of what was passing away. But their minds were made dull, for to this day, the same veil remains when the old covenant is read. It has not been removed, because only in Christ is it taken away" Corinthians 3:12-14.

4. Love Selflessly

Love God with all your heart. Know that He is the one who has made you, and He is the one who can change things for the better for you. So love Him, and form that unbreakable bond with him. Everything in life is temporary. It is only God who is permanent. He is the one who will be there with us till the very end, so love Him more than anyone else. Prioritize Him over everyone else, and listen to what He has said. Build that bond with him where you are content with everything in your life, only because you think that this was God's commandment. Building that bond with God can take some time. You will only be able to feel His presence once you make that conscious effort to do so. Set a time for praying every day, and do what God tells you to do. When you follow his commandments, you will see how things automatically start becoming so much better for you.

In every relationship that you have, be giving. Love the ones who are dear to you selflessly, and you will see how your relationships grow with them. The people I love the most in the world are my grandkids, and I can safely say that seeing them bloom into such lovely people gives me more happiness than anything else. I love them with all my heart, and I can see how much they love me too. Give everything you have in a relationship without expecting too much in return. That is the key to staying happy. When you do that, you will see how things turn out in your favor. God has time and again stressed the importance of selflessness and loving each other. In the Bible, he says "You should have the same attitude toward one another that Christ Jesus had, who though he existed in the form of God did not regard equality with God as something to be grasped, but emptied himself by taking on the form of a slave, by looking like other men, and by sharing in human nature. He humbled himself, by becoming obedient to the point of death, even death on a cross!" Philippians 2:5-8.

5. Have a Winning Mindset

I cannot stress enough the importance of having a winning mindset. When you have a winning mindset, you can achieve anything you set your head to. The opportunities for learning and growth are then endless, and they help you take that step towards success. How you think impacts your life greatly and helps you plan your future. I remember when I was in the hospital thinking that I wouldn't make it, I told myself that if I didn't have that winning mindset, how would I ever make it? So I tried to be positive and told myself I would surely come out of this if God wanted me to. And so, I did.

You see, the first step to achieving what you want is to believe that you can. It is to train your mind in a way that you focus on the good and understand how vital it is to move in that direction.

You need to find out what motivates you, and then you need to hold on to it to keep moving ahead in a certain direction. Remember that roadblocks will all be a part of life. You must understand what it means to keep moving forward, despite the roadblocks. That winning mindset will help you achieve more than you ever think you can.

6. Fight For Your Future

Who doesn't wish to have a better future for themselves, right? But if you want a better future, you must fight for it. You must do everything you can to change your life. If you think things in your life aren't going how you wanted them to, try to change them for the better. Work hard and be in control of your life. Try to do all you can to eliminate all the negatives in your life. To get a better life, you must understand that you have to do what you can to help yourself. God has plans for you, but you need to be the one to fight and get there. You have to put in the hard work, and then you will see how God's help automatically follows. The only being you should have expectations from is God because He is the one who gets things done. He is the one who has ultimate control over things. Stop expecting people to do things for you because it only leads to setbacks which can eventually put you down and take you to a dark place.

7. Stop Complaining

More often than not, people lament about their lives and how they aren't being able to get what they want. They lament failed plans and unsuccessful efforts. To live a happy and peaceful life, you need to stop complaining. You need to do your best to get what you want. Focus on what lies ahead of you rather than what you could have gotten but didn't. To live a happy and peaceful life is the most important thing. Try to be content with what God has given you, and you will see how you automatically get so much peace. According to the Bible, "Do not be anxious about anything, but in every situation, by prayer and petition, with thanksgiving, present your requests to God. And the peace of God, which transcends all understanding, will guard your hearts and your minds in Christ Jesus" Philippians 4:6-7.

8. Be Goal-Oriented

To get somewhere in life, you need to have goals. These goals can be anything. But when you set your mind to something, try to do your best to get there by having everything planned out correctly. My goal in life is to form a connection with God and have God as my number one. I have been working towards this goal for a very long time and have taken all the required steps to achieve this. So you must set a goal for yourself and also envision yourself getting there. When you do that, the motivation to keep giving your best to what you are doing goes up, allowing you to understand your life in a much better way. A life with a purpose is always the best life because it allows you to continuously focus on improving and getting better with time. It allows you to slowly work your way up, which is necessary if you wish to live a successful life. According to the Bible, "For we are God's handiwork, created in Christ Jesus to do good works, which God prepared in advance for us to do." Ephesians 2-10.

9. Never Give Up

In situations where we feel like things aren't working out the way we wanted, we tend to give up. We tend to let go of the slightest bit of hope that we had. This is the worst thing that you can do to yourself. You can only get what you want in life when you keep trying hard for it and give your hundred percent without fail. When you give up, you stop trying, and that is where the downfall starts. Understand that roadblocks are a natural part of life. They will surely come. You have to be the one to look ahead of those roadblocks and get your life sorted. Even if things seem very difficult, believe in God and know that He will give you the strength to keep going because He is the one who has control over everything in life. The Bible says, "And Jesus answered them, "Have faith in God. Truly, I say to you, whoever says to this mountain, 'Be taken up and thrown into the sea,' and does not doubt in his heart but believes that what he says will come to pass, it will be done for him. Therefore I tell you, whatever you ask in prayer, believe that you have received it, and it will be yours" Mark 11:22-24.

10.Be Humble

I cannot stress enough the importance of being humble in life. Humility is one of the most important attributes of growth. It allows you to understand others, be compassionate, and remain grounded. Pride only leads to downfall. So try your best, help others, let God take control of things, and see how things turn for the better for you.

Whenever someone criticizes you, understand why they're saying that and take it as constructive criticism so that you can improve and further work on yourself. Whenever you make a mistake, apologize and try not to do it again. Time and again, God has stressed the importance of apologizing. He says, "Confess your sins to each other and pray for each other so that you may be healed. The earnest prayer of a righteous person has great power and produces wonderful results: James 5:16.

When you are humble, you will be able to build more confidence too, which will allow you to work harder and get a step closer to your goals each day. When you are humble, you also build more meaningful relationships because others like to be with you. They love the energy you spread. Humble people also have the desire to keep learning. Remember that we are all humans and that there is always something new to learn.

11.Be Open to Learning

These days, whenever someone tries to tell us something, we rarely pay heed to it. We think that we know more than they do. The truth is that this only comes from a place of sheer arrogance. We are all creatures of knowledge, and we learn all our lives. To keep learning is the key to living a fulfilled life. Only God is the one who is all-powerful and all-knowing. Only He is the one who has ultimate knowledge about all things. We are his people who need to keep learning and understanding things as they come our way. The Bible says, "The revelation of Jesus Christ, which God gave him to show to his servants the things that must soon take place. He made it known by sending his angel to his servant John, who bore witness to the word of God and to the testimony of Jesus Christ, even to all that he saw. Blessed is the one who reads aloud the words of this prophecy, and blessed are those who hear and who keep what is written in it, for the time is near. John to the seven churches that are in Asia: Grace to you and peace from him who is and who was and who is to come, and from the seven spirits who are before his throne, and from Jesus Christ the faithful witness, the firstborn of the dead, and the ruler of kings on earth. To him who loves us and has freed us from our sins by his blood" Revelation 1:1-20.

No matter how knowledgeable we are, there is always more room for learning, which makes us improve. No matter how old or what stage of life you are in, you can always learn more and understand things in much more detail. I am at a stage of my life where I have grandchildren. But even at this stage of life, I am learning new things each day. I love how it is helping me evolve as a person and understand things in a much better way too. Learning aids growth and development, allowing us to boost our confidence and further work on our abilities.

12.Be Patient

Try to be as patient as you can. Good things only come to those who wait. If you are trying to get something in life, work hard for it, but also understand that it won't come to you just because you want it. It can take some time for things to unfold. You need to be patient with it. Keep trying and giving your best to what you are doing, but understand that it can take time. God has repeatedly stressed the importance of being patient in life. In the Bible, He says, "Let us not become weary in doing good, for at the proper time we will reap a harvest if we do not give up" Galatians 6:9.

When we're patient, it helps us reduce all negative emotions and allows us to deal with stress much better. It also allows us to make informed decisions after evaluating all our options. Not only that, but it enables us to work well with other people around. Patience brings out the best in us. When we take our own time to evaluate our options and understand things much better, we can work our way through everything. Not just that, but we can also focus on the good in life. It allows us to learn from our mistakes and do things for the better.

I can safely say that I have wanted to develop a strong relationship with God for a long time now. I was very patient with it throughout, and slowly and gradually, things started working out for me. It took some time, but today, I have a very strong relationship with God, and I couldn't be more thankful for it. God has helped me transform myself because I was patient and worked hard to get what I wanted. The one thing that I didn't ever let go of was prayer. I kept asking God for all that I wanted, and He indeed did give it to me. I believe in the power of prayer more than anything else, and I can say that God helped me with everything. God has time and again stressed the importance of prayer in life. He says, "Is anyone among you sick? Let him call for the elders of the church, and let them pray over him, anointing him with oil in the name of the Lord. And the prayer of faith will save the one who is sick, and the Lord will raise him up. And if he has committed sins, he will be forgiven. Therefore, confess your sins to one another and pray that you may be healed. The prayer of a righteous person has great power as it is working" James 5:14-16.

So, you must always be patient. When you wait for something, you will see that the return you get for it will also be very rewarding. Have faith and trust in God's plans, and you will see how they turn out for the better. You will get rewarded for your patience in this life and the hereafter.

13.Stop Comparing Yourself to Others

Seeking validation is very common these days. We also tend to look at others around us and compare ourselves to them. That is the worst thing you can do for your mental health.

Social media, in part, has led to false and unreal ideals that continuously make us believe that we aren't good enough. No one is as good as social media makes them look, but very few understand this. We look at others around us and compare ourselves to them, which inculcates negative feelings inside of us, making us feel inadequate. Remember that you are unique. God has made you, and He has chosen the best for you. So you need to make sure that you focus on yourself. For your well-being and mental health, focus on all God has given you and see how better off you are than the rest. Never forget that God loves you, and you are one of His most precious creations. So focus on that the most.

In the Bible, God says, "Can anything ever separate us from Christ's love? Does it mean He no longer loves us if we have trouble or calamity, or are persecuted, or hungry, or destitute, or in danger, or threatened with death? ... No, despite all these things, overwhelming victory is ours through Christ, who loved us. And I am convinced that nothing can ever separate us from God's love. Neither death nor life, neither angels nor demons, neither our fears for today nor our worries about tomorrow — not even the powers of hell can separate us from God's love. No power in the sky above or in the earth below — indeed, nothing in all creation will ever be able to separate us from the love of God that is revealed in Christ Jesus our Lord" Romans 8:35, 37-39   .

The only comparison you should be making is between the person you were yesterday and the person you are today. That will help you improve yourself even further. It will help you get more clarity on things too, which means that you will be able to focus on continuous improvement. Time and again, God has stressed the importance of improving ourselves each passing day. So we must focus on the present, work on our weaknesses, and plan to get better with time.

Looking back in time, I can point out so many things that I wasn't good at. But I made it a point to focus on improving. I worked on my weak points each day because I wanted to become better as a person. I wanted to follow each commandment that God has given, so when I look back, I can safely say that I have come a long way. I have improved my relationship with God by overcoming my weak points and making a conscious effort to obey Him.

14.Step Out of Your Comfort Zone

When we do something for a continuous time repeatedly, we get used to it. We tend to then feel comfortable doing that. Your growth only begins when you step out of your comfort zone and strive harder to achieve what you want. Initially, it might seem like quite a task, but you will eventually see how much it helps you achieve. Each time you step out of your comfort zone with a goal in mind, you get one step closer to achieving it.

Remember that change is inevitable in life. When you step out of your comfort zone, you become much better equipped to manage that change in the right way. It helps you stay calmer when dealing with the unknown. Throughout my life, I have been someone who never liked to step out of my comfort zone for anything at all. It was only when I did that, that I realized how helpful it was and how much it helped me. It gave me a new perspective on things, allowing me to understand all I was heading towards fully.

15.Be Kind to Others

Kindness, again, is a godly virtue. You never know how far one act of kindness can go. Even if it only manages to bring a smile to one person's face, consider your job done. With so much cruelty in the world, kindness needs to become more widespread to inculcate positivity. So try to be as kind to others as you can. Even if someone is mean to you, don't respond back in a mean way. Be nice to them, hoping that they too will understand the importance of being kind someday. Kindness helps bring feelings of positivity around and also helps you see the bright side of things. God has also stressed the importance of being kind. In the Bible, God says, "And if anyone would sue you and take your tunic, let him have your cloak as well. And if anyone forces you to go one mile, go with him two miles. Give to the one who begs from you, and does not refuse the one who would borrow from you. You have heard that it is said, 'You shall love your neighbor and hate your enemy.' But I say to you, love your enemies and pray for those who persecute you" Matthew 5:40-43.

We all have to coexist. We won't always have the same opinions of things. What is important is that we need to be kind to each other to make the world a much better place. It is always easy to let your anger out on someone else. It is harder to learn how to deal with it correctly and how that can help you contribute to making the world a better place.

16.Control Your Anger

One of the most negative emotions is anger. When you're angry, you tend to lose the ability to think straight and do things you wouldn't do otherwise. It can damage your relationships and even cause harm to those around you. So, you must make a conscious effort to control your anger before your anger starts controlling you. In the Bible. God has been clear about why controlling anger is important and what damage it can lead to. He says, "But be doers of the word, and not hearers only, deceiving yourselves. For if anyone is a hearer of the word and not a doer, he is like a man who looks intently at his natural face in a mirror. For he looks at himself, goes away, and at once forgets what he was like. But the one who looks into the perfect law, the law of liberty, and perseveres, being no hearer who forgets but a doer who acts, he will be blessed in his doing. If anyone thinks he is religious and does not bridle his tongue but deceives his heart, this person's religion is worthless" James 1:22-27.

If you struggle with anger issues, you must learn anger management by first understanding yourself and what triggers you. Then, whenever you are angry, try to remove yourself from that situation. Pause and take a deep breath. Have some water and try to make a conscious effort to relax. When you do that, you will surely see yourself slowly calming down. However, for the best anger management, you need to learn what works for you, which can only happen when you understand yourself well.

17.Don't Backbite

As human beings, it's very common for us to point out other people's faults and then talk about them behind their backs. This is the worst thing you can do. It is also one of the greatest sins. Think of it this way: if the other person finds out about what you were saying about them, wouldn't it hurt them? Also, is backbiting making your life any better? Then why do something that is only creating negativity? Remember that you are only responsible for your own actions. You need to have answers for what you do. So remember that speaking ill about someone else only reflects badly on you, adding to your sins. The more you focus on your growth, the better you become as a person, which is what you need to do to make your life more fulfilled.

I remember I was once sitting with a few friends when one of them started talking about another friend. Since I was sitting with them, I also became an active contributor to the conversation without realizing what I was doing. It was only much later, when I thought about what I was doing, that I realized how wrong I was. I swore that I would never backbite again. You never know what someone has gone through or what their relationship with God is like. They might even be much better than you. Only God knows what is in people's hearts. So focus on that, and try to get better each passing day. You will see how much that helps and how you transform into a much better person.

The Bible also has very specific commandments about backbiting, prohibiting it under all circumstances. God says, "Judge not, that you be not judged. For with the judgment, you pronounce, you will be judged, and with the measure, you use it will be measured to you. Why do you see the speck that is in your brother's eye, but do not notice the log that is in your own eye? Or how can you say to your brother, 'Let me take the speck out of your eye,' when there is the log in your own eye? You hypocrite, first take the log out of your own eye, and then you will see clearly to take the speck out of your brother's eye" Matthew 7:1-5.

18.Take Care of Your Health

There is no bigger blessing than health. If you don't have any serious medical issues and don't have to visit the doctor often, consider yourself very lucky. Most people don't have what you have. Be thankful for your health since it is the biggest blessing God has given. Not just that, but also be careful with what you eat and how active you keep yourself.

Think of it this way- there are so many things that we take for granted, such as whether we can swallow food down our throat or defecate. This is because God has blessed us with the gift of health. It is because of this gift that we are able to do so much with our lives. So focus on that and thank God every day for His blessings. Not just that, but also focus on what you eat. Try to eat a balanced diet and also stay active as much as you can. This isn't just about you but also about pleasing God, who has blessed you with the gift of health.

Try to get regular checkups done to make sure that you are doing alright. Not just that, but also focus on developing healthier habits early on in life so you don't have to suffer when you grow old. Stop eating anything that is bad for you, especially all that God has forbidden you from consuming. When you listen to God and thank Him for his blessings, you will see how much your life changes for the better and how that allows you to do better each day.

According to the Bible, "Do you not know that your bodies are temples of the Holy Spirit, who is in you, whom you have received from God? You are not your own; you were bought at a price. Therefore, honor God with your bodies" Corinthians 6:19-20.

19.Never Envy Others

There is no end to our desires. So whenever we see someone doing better than us, it is only natural for us to feel a sense of envy. We are all human, and it is alright to look up to people.

However, envy is a very strong negative feeling. So you need to make sure that you stay away from it. Whenever you see someone better off than you, pray for them and praise the Lord who has enabled them to get there. Don't let feelings of jealousy take over. When you do that, you inculcate negativity within yourself. So focus on becoming better. If you like something they have or if you like what they have become, pray to God. Praying is the solution to everything. When you do that, God will bless you, giving you more than you ever wished for.

But when you are envious and have negative feelings brewing up inside you, it deprives you of the good in life and makes you a negative person. So every time you feel envious, try to let go of all of those negative feelings to become a much better person.

When you envy others, you also spend a lot of your energy doing something negative, barely leaving you with any room to focus on the good in life. Not just that, but it also tends to make you more hostile towards others around you. It exhausts you mentally and is more than just hazardous for your mental health.

God has laid down very specific commandments about envy. In the Bible, he says, "But if you have bitter jealousy and selfish ambition in your hearts, do not boast and be false to the truth. This is not the wisdom that comes down from above but is earthly, unspiritual, and demonic. For where jealousy and selfish ambition exist, there will be disorder and every vile practice" James 3:14-16.

So focus on positive things. When you do that, you become so much more beautiful on the inside that it starts reflecting on the outside too. The ultimate goal is to become a better person, and when you let go of all these feelings, you can also work on that.

20.Mind Your Own Business

Most people I know poke their noses in other people's business. This is one of the worst traits one can have.

When you mind your own business, you are much more productive, which allows you to focus on the good in life. It allows you to have a 'live and let live approach, which is extremely important to help you grow. When you are intrusive, others don't like to be around you. They see you as an extremely toxic person who gives unsolicited advice to others.

Speaking from personal experience, I have this friend who had the habit of looking around to see what others were doing. He didn't do this out of concern or to help, but rather out of habit. We all disliked being around that specific friend because he embodied negative energy.

In today's times, most people need to understand the importance of minding their own businesses and being concerned with only what they have on their own plate. When they do that, they will surely be able to earn respect from others. Not just that, but other people will also like to be around them.

21.Live and Let Live

This is the biggest life lesson I want to give those around me. Live in the moment because this life is the biggest blessing that God has given us. Make every moment count. Even when things don't go your way, understand that this is God's way of bringing you close to Him.

When you do that, you will realize how there is so much you have to look forward to. Cherish this gift that God has given you, and understand that nothing can go wrong with God's presence and love in your life.

In the Bible, God has repeatedly focused on how this life is a huge blessing. He says, "And whatever you do, in word or deed, do everything in the name of the Lord Jesus, giving thanks to God the Father through him" Colossians 3:17.

Not only should you live your life to the fullest, but you should also let others live peacefully. Your being should not cause trouble to anyone around you. You should be a source of comfort to those around you, meaning that you should never let the other person feel like you're imposing something on them. Live by your beliefs and let them live by theirs. It will surely bring them a lot of peace and will help you live peacefully too, knowing that you helped others get what they wanted.

My idea here isn't to sound too preachy. I just want to impart what I have learned to those around me because I take this on as my responsibility. I want as many people as possible to benefit from the life lessons I have to offer so they can improve the quality of their lives too.

With these life lessons, I hope you can get what you want and work your way through life successfully.

Chapter 8: God- The Ultimate Love

As I near the end of this book, I want everyone to feel this sense of closeness to God, where they understand what it means to feel God near you. Your one true love will always be God. Think of the many times we human beings sin.

Each time we go back to Him, knowing that He is our only hope, He accepts us. He forgives us for all our sins. Yet, we sin again, and again, and again. Each time, He welcomes us with open arms. Why? Because God loves us more than anyone else. God has made us, and so He is the one who knows us inside out. He knows what each of us is made of, and he is aware of our characteristics too.

There are many people I know who hesitate to turn back to God, thinking that He won't forgive them. But that is surely not the case. You should never let your sins hold you back from God.

It is important to understand that God is waiting for you to turn to Him. He wants you to turn to Him and ask for whatever you want. He will be there to give you all of that because He loves you. His love is incomparable to human love. It transcends everything human, and we need to understand that. Whatever we are today is because of His love.

Whenever I try to imagine the extent to which God loves me, I think of it this way: I got into very tragic and scary incidents in my life. Once I got shot. Then, I got into a terrible accident while riding my bike. I could have lost my life. If not, I could have lost one of my limbs and would have spent my life in a wheelchair. Such a life would have been incredibly difficult for me. I may not have found it worth living. It was God who saved me from that life. He was the one to give me another life, and I cannot be more thankful to Him for this gift.

In my case, when I realized how much God loves me, I understood the meaning of life. I understood that nothing mattered to me more than God. Anything could have happened to me, but here I am, doing perfectly fine, writing this book and sharing my life experiences with everyone. I consider this nothing short of a blessing for myself. I think God has been very kind to me. He saved me from so many disasters that could have happened. Why? Because He loves me. I was about to die. To date, I don't understand how I got saved. It does not matter anyway. What matters is that it was God who saved me. He loves me more than anyone else, and so I also feel immense loyalty toward God.

Slowly and gradually, I built this relationship with God since He is the one I look up to for everything. Every time I feel troubled, I look up to God. I ask Him for help, and He helps me with everything.

Whenever I feel bogged down, I ask God for help, and He helps me.

The most important message I want to give everyone is that the key to a successful life is building a relationship with God. When you do that, nothing in your life can go wrong because you understand that God is the one who is in control of everything in your life. God has everything planned for you beforehand. Even when you don't get something you have asked for, understand that God knew that it wasn't good for you since He is All-knowing.

More often than not, I have seen people losing faith when things don't turn out the way they want. They lose hope, and they stop doing the things that they should focus on with respect to their relationship with God. When you ask God for something, do it with conviction, knowing that He will only give it to you if it is the best for you. Know that He loves you more than anyone else and has bestowed you with the best in life. So if He isn't giving you something you want, it is probably the best for you because we don't know what He knows since he is the controller of the world.

Time and again, the Bible has focused on this attribute of God. "For the word of God is living and active and sharper than any two-edged sword, and piercing as far as the division of soul and spirit, of both joints and marrow, and able to judge the thoughts and intentions of the heart. And there is no creature hidden from His sight, but all things are open and laid bare to the eyes of Him with whom we have to do" Hebrews 4:12-13.

This life is a beautiful gift from God, so cherish it. Your life will become even more beautiful with God's presence in it. When you connect yourself to God, you will see how you have this contentment and peace in your heart that no one else does. You will see how nothing will trouble you as much because you will always know that God is there for you and has planned everything in a way that is in your best interest. You will know that nothing in your life can happen unless God orders it to happen. So with this in your heart, you will be able to focus on Him. It is a two-way connection.

Whenever I ask God for something, I do so in isolation. It is only Him and me. I feel that deep connection with God, and I feel like He is listening to whatever I am telling Him. That feeling only gets stronger when it continues to happen over time. For all those struggling with one thing or the other in life, I want to tell you that the key to happiness is building that bond with God. I can testify how this has worked for me and turned my life around in a way I could never have imagined. It has made me so content on the inside that no matter what happens, I never get bogged down easily.

Many people struggle with developing that bond with God because somewhere inside, they believe they will not be able to do it. The key is to understand that God is always waiting for you. He wants you to turn to Him. I view all hardships as obstacles that come our way, just to remind us that He is there waiting for us and the only one who can help us through our hardships. The sooner we understand this, the better it is for us. When we turn to God once, he becomes so happy knowing that we remembered Him, knowing that only He is the one who can help us through all types of hardship.

When you turn to other people for help, you will see that it won't help you much. Other people are never of too much help anyway. God, on the other hand, is always there to help you. He is always there to give you what you want. It is only us who need to turn to Him for everything. When we do that, we will see that help will come itself.

Getting Close to God

Now that you know why getting close to God is important and how it can improve your life, here are a few tips that can help you with that.

- **Feel His Presence**

God is always there. You need to feel his presence everywhere and in whatever you do. To feel his presence, sit quietly in a place without any of your electronic devices. Put everything aside and notice all that is happening around you. The moon, the stars, the little babies being born, the hustle and bustle all over. What does it hint to? Doesn't it tell you that there is a Supreme Being who is controlling all of this?

Doesn't this tell you that He is the one who will always be there and is the one who has been there from the beginning of times? When you notice all of this, you will surely be able to see that God is omnipresent.

- **Read the Scripture**

The scripture is God's message to all of us where He conveys his thoughts to us. He guides us about everything in life through his messages in the Bible. The scripture can offer guidance on even the littlest of things.

The Holy Book should be your guide in life. A few years back, whenever any problem came my way, I would get very upset, not knowing the best way out of the issue. Then I started consulting the scripture and I felt like every single verse was speaking to me, giving me the solution to my problem. This is exactly what you need to do as well. Make it a point to have a set routine in a way that you read the scripture daily. When you do that, you will see how sorted your life becomes. It worked very well for me, and I want all my readers to benefit from this.

- **Pray**

As obvious as it seems, praying is the one thing that connects you the most with God. When you are in prayer, it is only you and Him, one to one. In that time, connect with God as deeply as you can. If you have any other thoughts in your head, let go of all of them. Only think about God and your connection with Him. Submit your soul to God and be immersed in His remembrance. When you do that, your prayer will automatically become very different. It will help you connect with God in a very different way. It will help you understand what it means to speak one-on-one with God. When in prayer, ask God for anything you want or need.

God will be there to listen to you and solve all your problems all at once. When asking God for something, do it with full conviction, believing that He is there to listen to every word you utter. It is through His hand over you that you have been able to reach so far and get things done your way.

God has focused on the importance of praying time and again in the Bible. He says, "Do not be anxious about anything, but in every situation, by prayer and petition, with thanksgiving, present your requests to God. And the peace of God transcends all understanding, will guard your hearts and minds in Christ Jesus" Philippians 4:6-7.

- **Share God's Words with Others**

Religion is not only about praying and communicating with God. It is about spreading the word of God to others as well, who can benefit from it. When you do this, you will see how much satisfaction it gives you. If someone gets closer to God or starts praying because of you, you will also be rewarded for that. God will be pleased with you because you spread His message to others.

- **Love Others**

Earlier in this book, I mentioned the importance of spreading love everywhere. Religion is all about love. It is about loving others unconditionally and spreading positivity everywhere. When you do that, you will see how great you feel on the inside, which is what you need to get closer to God. When you help people and love them with all your heart, God rewards you.

- **Count Your Blessings**

Count all that God has bestowed you with every day. When you do that, you will see how much God loves you and how He is with you in every step. You will automatically love God more when seeing how He has transformed your life. It is God who is the one to help you with everything.

- **Spend Time with Knowledgeable People**

When you spend time with those who have ample knowledge of the scripture, you will see how that knowledge gets passed on to you. Spending time with such people allows you to understand God so much better. These people have so much valuable knowledge to impart.

So, my friends, your journey to becoming closer to God starts today. Slowly but surely, you will get there. When you get closer to God, you will see how much it will help you. You will feel a drastic change in your life when you get close to God. You will have His remembrance with you in everything you do, which is what you need to grow and become better.

Love. Light. Repentance. Goodness.

Live by this motto, and you will see what your life becomes. I hope and pray that each one of you gets what you want in life, and that God is with you in each step that you take. I wish nothing less than love and light for you.

About the Author

Maurice M. Jenkins is a resident of Racine, Wisconsin. He was born and brought up in Jackson, Mississippi. He went to Pearl High School and Murrah High School for his early education and graduated from Gateway College. He then went on to enlist in the US Army before retiring in 2012.

As a retired US Army veteran, he wants to share his life experiences with readers, and give them a message about building a relationship with God and why it matters. The author is very passionate about this topic and aims to spread more awareness about it through his work.

He is a father to three kids and a grandfather to two. He spends most of his free time with his family.